I0829492

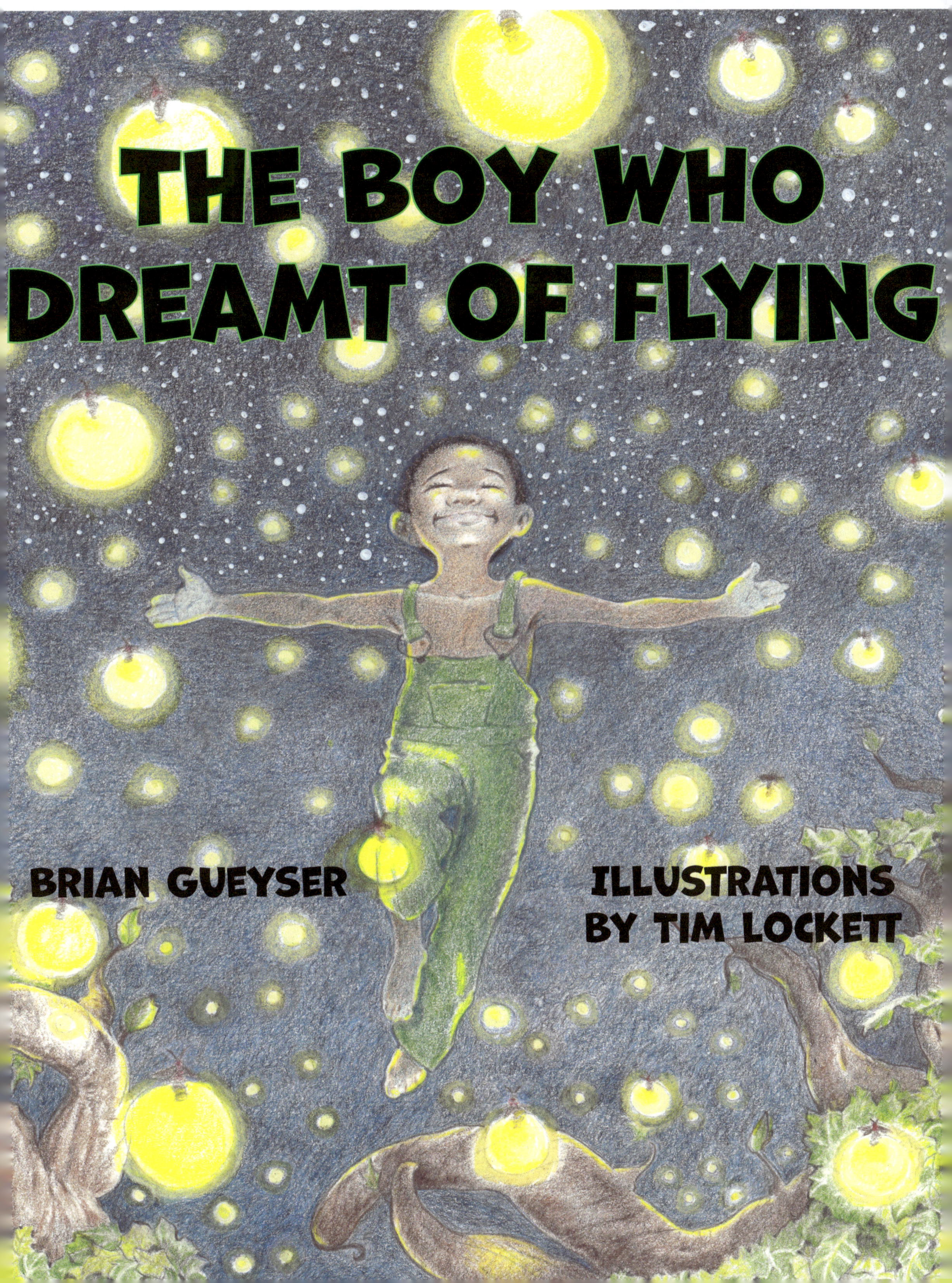

THE BOY WHO DREAMT OF FLYING
BRIAN GUEYSER
ILLUSTRATIONS BY TIM LOCKETT

Kids At Heart Publishing LLC
PO Box 492
Milton, IN 47357
765-478-5773
www.kidsatheartpublishing.com

Published by Kids At Heart Publishing LLC May 31, 2022.

ISBN 978-1-956628-06-7
Library of Congress Control Number: 2022904217

Published in Milton, Indiana, and
printed in Indiana.

This book is printed on acid-free paper.

To order more copies of this book go to
www.kidsatheartpublishing.com.

Kids At Heart Publishing LLC books feature "Turn the Page Technology."
No batteries or charging required.

Dedication

To the part of each and every one of us
which longs for the freedom of flight…
keep soaring!

There once was a boy who dreamt of flying.

He saw the birds soaring through the air, and saw the clouds as they floated along and he always felt as if somewhere UP THERE was his true home.

His favorite part of the daily walk to school was watching the sky. He loved to see the clouds reflected in the large puddles the rainwater would create … as if making a giant jigsaw puzzle only he could see.

When it was kite-flying season, and the winds would blow, he would run through the fields with his arms stretched wide, waiting…always just on the edge of— what he was sure—being carried back to where he truly belonged.

When grown-ups asked him what he wanted
to do when he grew up, he always told them he
wanted to fly. But they never understood him.
"On a plane?" he would hear them ask time
after time. "Oh you'd make such a wonderful
pilot! You must be very brave," they'd say.

One day his mother asked him what he wanted to do when he grew up. He told her he wanted to fly.

"I think it's wonderful you want to be a pilot," she said, "but you'll have to do your very best in school so that you can learn to fly airplanes." When he told her what he meant, her face changed. "Honey, people can't fly," she told him.

"But I've seen them," he replied.

His mother smiled. "Sweetie I know they show people flying on TV all by themselves and it seems real, but please remember what they show on television is only pretend. If you want to fly, you'll have to be a pilot, and learn to fly airplanes."

The boy was silent, and he cocked his head to the side as he considered her words. And from that day forward he began to understand that just because grown-ups were bigger did not mean that they were wise.

"Fly," came the voices, "fly," he heard someone calling as he sat up in the large maple tree watching the sky. "How?" he asked back, but there was no reply.

The boy became very observant. He knew that if he was to learn to fly, perhaps he should do so by watching the different creatures who flew around him every day.

And so, he watched the birds.

He watched the bees.

He watched the lightning bugs and danced
with them as they whispered in the dark...

He watched the dragonflies.

And he watched
the butterflies.

But most of all, he began to listen
with his heart.

He decided he was not like the birds, for he had no wings.

He decided he was not like the bees, because they only seemed concerned about flowers.

The dragonflies were mysterious. He knew they knew he was watching them. They flitted between the sunbeams and tried their best to trick him into following.

The lightning bugs claimed to keep secrets, but since they whispered to one another about just about everything, he soon learned that they could not teach him what he wanted to know.

But the butterflies…ah, yes, the butterflies. Perhaps they could help him, he reasoned.

He went to the fields and waited. Many butterflies came and went, but he knew that he would know the one to help him when he saw it. He knew she had arrived from the way she flew.

All the clovers and the reeds, the grasses and the stalks bent and swayed in the wind, yet she alone flew sturdy and strong. She was large, but not so large, and absolutely, unbelievably beautiful. She seemed to know that he was waiting, for she did not stop to gather nectar, but floated right before him.

"My dear Sister," the boy said, "thank you for coming. I need your help so that I may fly." The winds grew stronger, whipping and nipping at his pant-legs, and sending chills down the backs of his arms, but the butterfly calmly answered as she floated unwavering.

"Dear Child," she spoke, with words as sweet as pollen from summer fields of wildflowers, "Please understand that We only fly after great change. If you truly seek this knowledge, you also must be willing to transform."

That night as he lay in bed, he considered the Butterfly's words. How would he look when he transformed? He knew that before butterflies could fly, they were caterpillars. He wondered would his body shift and twist and bend until he became something completely unrecognizable.

He built his chrysalis out of
sheets and blankets, and
lined the inside with his
favorite drawings and toys.

He smiled as he fell
asleep, dreaming of
the transformation
that he was certain
would take place.

The next morning, he was
terribly disappointed.

"Fly," came the voices, "fly," he heard someone calling as he sat at his desk in school wishing he were outside in the air instead. "How?" he asked softly. And his teacher frowned, and told him to hush.

The boy decided to take his search to the library. He knew that libraries had many books, and that these books could teach you to cook, build things, or even learn another language! If he could only find the proper books, he reasoned, he should be flying in no time.

When he explained to the librarian what he was looking for, she smiled down kindly at him. Then she led him down the aisles into the section for grown-ups. There at the top of a tall bookshelf, was a large book with a soft blue color.

He hefted the book into his arms, and went straight to an empty table so he could begin studying. As he poured over the book's pages, he began to frown. He took the book back to the librarian. "This book teaches you how to leave your body," he explained, "I already do this at night when I dream." The librarian was very astonished by his words, but quietly took the book back and watched him leave.

"Fly," came the voices. "Fly" he heard someone calling as he sat down to eat dinner that night. "LEAVE ME ALONE!" he shouted back at them. "What's gotten into you?!" his mother asked, surprised. But he looked down at the table, and would not answer her.

One day at school, his teacher informed the class that they would have to give a speech about what they wanted to do when they grew up. They had one week to prepare, she told them.

The little boy was very
excited about his speech,
and spent the next week
preparing it very carefully…
making sure to choose the
proper words, and writing
extra-slowly so that his
handwriting would be neat
and beautiful.

He even practiced his speech out loud, making sure to speak loudly and clearly so that everyone could hear and understand him.

When it finally came time to
give his speech, he was ready.
He gave a big smile and read in
his loudest inside voice so that
even the students in the back of
the classroom could hear him.

WHEN I GROW UP

He spoke about the way the clouds moved, and how he imagined they would feel against his skin when he went racing through them. He spoke about the way the birds chased each other, and how he imagined himself playing wonderful games of tag with them. He spoke about how he imagined the stars would look when he was dancing in the air among them. He spoke about how he wanted to fly.

When he was finished, the
class clapped politely and
his teacher smiled, but later
that day at recess, something
awful happened.

"There he is, look!" he heard someone saying, "There's that stupid kid who thinks he can fly!" "Hey birdbrain!" they called at him, "show us what you can do!"

He tried to ignore them, but they wouldn't go away, and soon they had surrounded him. "Don't you know that people can't fly," they told him. "Yea dummy," another one said, "only birds and insects can fly. What are you stupid?!" The little boy looked for the matrons who were supposed to be watching them, but they were nowhere to be found.

"What's the matter, can't you talk?" they asked, taunting him. When he didn't respond, they began to push and shove him. Soon they were kicking and hitting him. He covered his head with his arms and curled into a little ball. He imagined himself high above, soaring through the air.

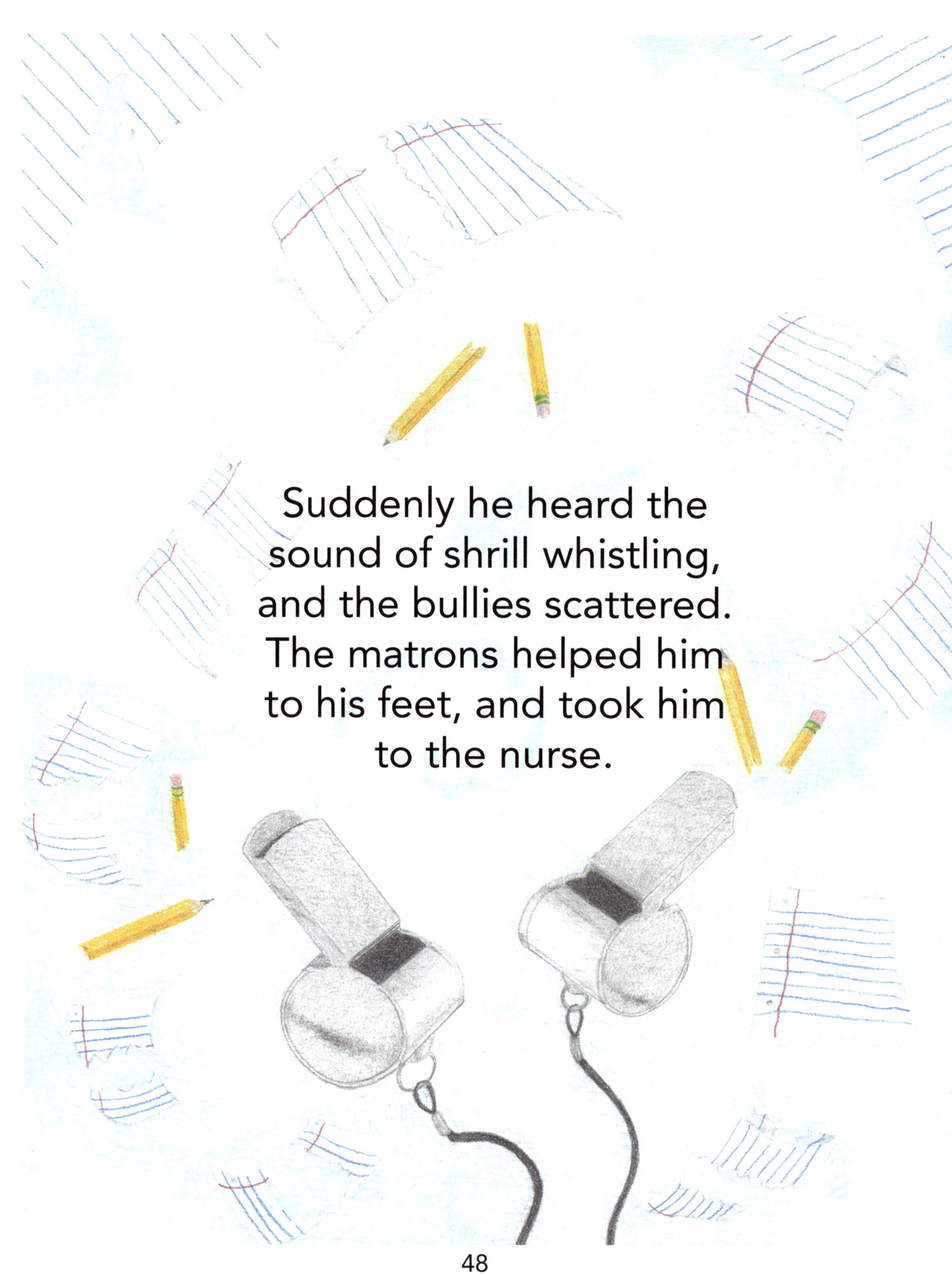

Suddenly he heard the
sound of shrill whistling,
and the bullies scattered.
The matrons helped him
to his feet, and took him
to the nurse.

"What happened?" she asked kindly, and he burst into tears and fled out the door. He ran down the hallway and before long he was outside again. He kept running and running, as fast as his legs would carry him, until he found himself in his own neighborhood at his own door.

He pounded and pounded, and when his mother finally came to see who it was, she was very surprised. "What on Earth! Oh my goodness!" she cried out in fright.

When he told her what happened, she grew very angry. She snatched up her keys, and took him by the hand.

Then she drove them right back to the school where she barged into the office. "JUST WHAT KIND OF IRRESPONSIBLE ANIMALS DO YOU THINK YOU ARE?!" she shouted.

The secretaries grew wide-eyed, and quickly ushered the boy out into the hall, where he sat and waited in the orange chairs for bad kids. While he waited, he heard his mother screaming and shouting. He heard her pounding her fists on the office counter. He heard her calling the principal names he'd never heard his mother say before.

When she was finished, she took him by the hand and drove him home.

That night, they ate dinner in silence.

56

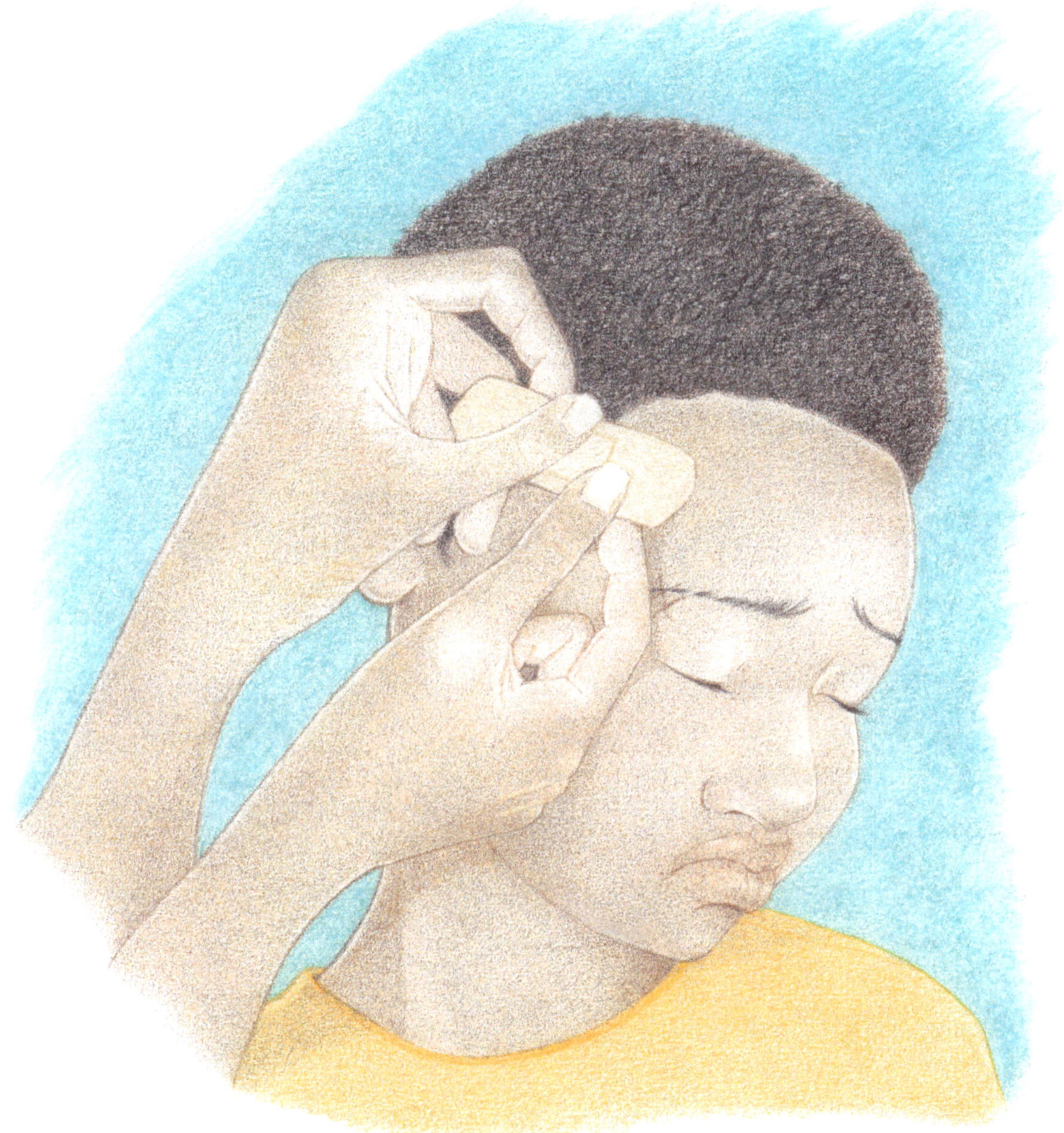

His mother put ice on his face, and bandaged his wounds. "Honey," she said softly, "I know you think you only want to fly, but I've told you it's not real. I'm very sorry for what happened today. But maybe if you stop pretending so much, you won't make them want to hurt you."

Then they went to bed early.

"Fly," came the voices. "Fly," he heard someone calling as he lay in bed trying his best to sleep. "Come and teach me," he said softly. Then he began to cry.

And he cried…

and cried…

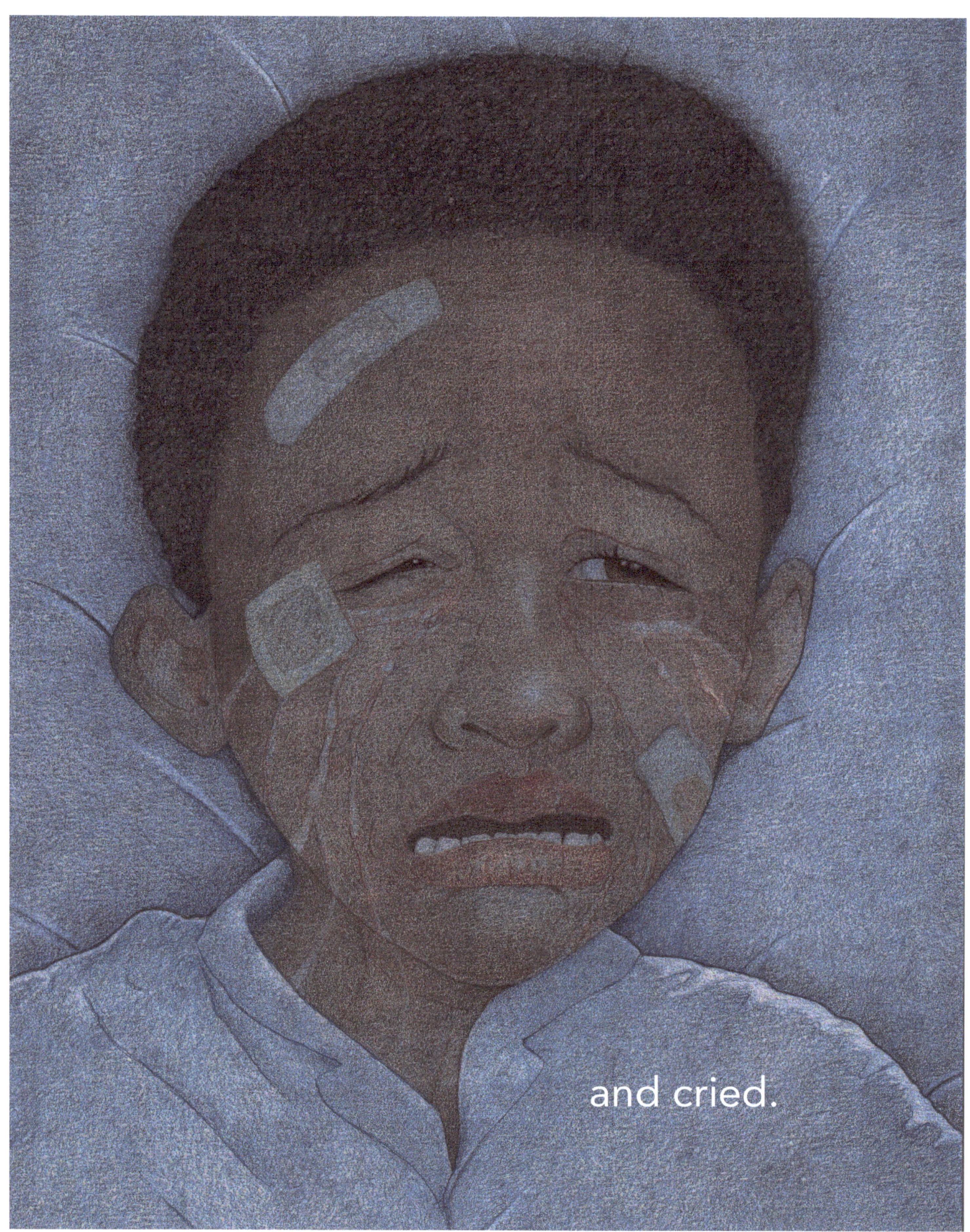
and cried.

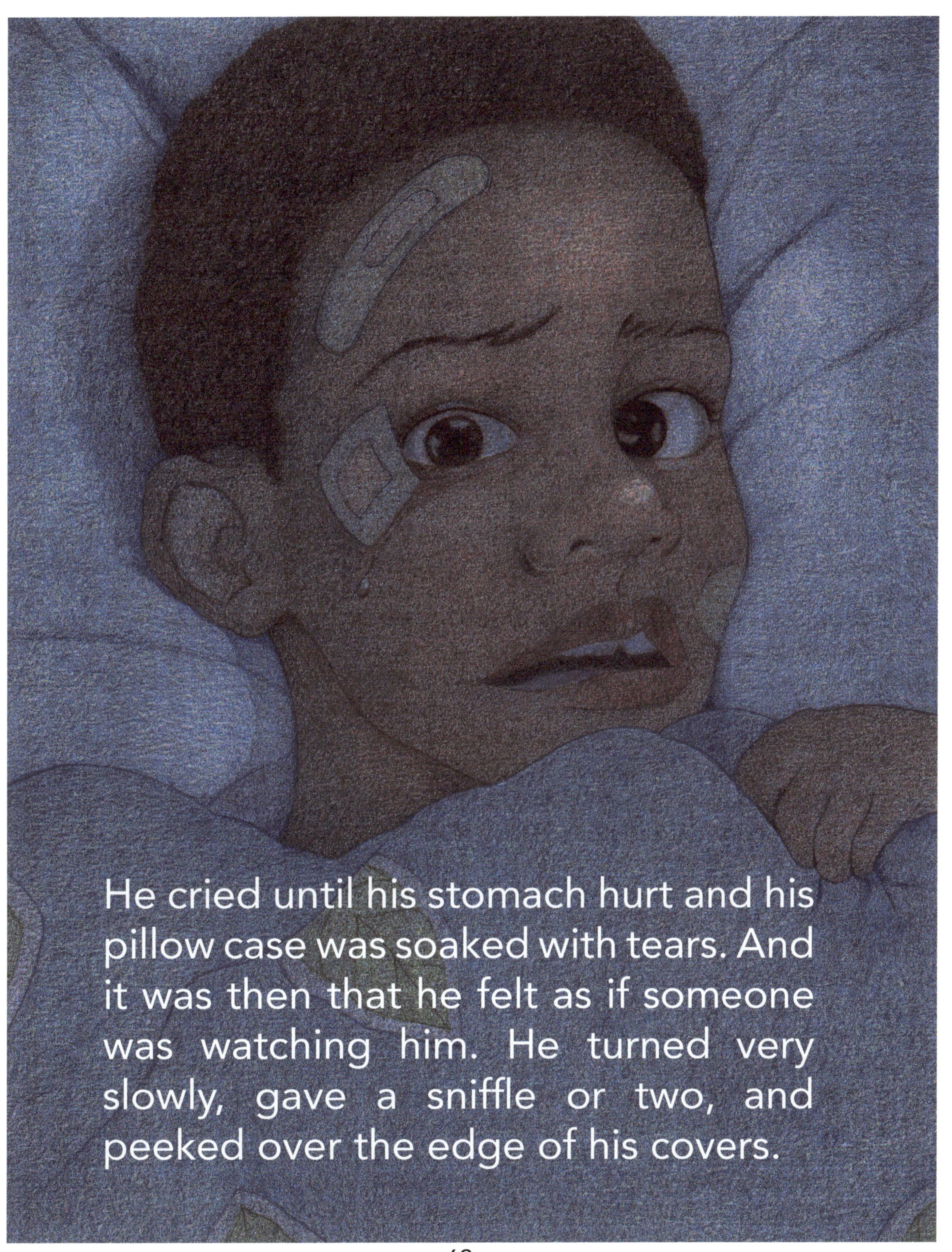

He cried until his stomach hurt and his pillow case was soaked with tears. And it was then that he felt as if someone was watching him. He turned very slowly, gave a sniffle or two, and peeked over the edge of his covers.

It only took a moment or two, and in the far corner over by the large armchair, he noticed a tall dark shadow.

The little boy sat up. He was very surprised. "Who are you?" he called out softly. "I know you're there. I can see you. What do you want?" he said.

"Little Boy, Little Boy, I've heard you want to fly," the shadow said. "Fly" came the echoes of many soft-cawed voices bouncing from the walls within and all around his room...except... it didn't quite seem like his room anymore. He wondered whether he was dreaming, but he knew he wasn't because it felt different.

The shadow moved closer, and as it did so he could see that this shadow was only a man dressed in a long, dark trench-coat. His dark hair was wild and tousled, his eyes bright and perceptive, his nose long and sharp. His skin browned and tanned as if he had spent many days in the hot sun.

On the floor near his bare feet were two long, black feathers. This made the little boy smile.

"I've heard you want to fly," the man repeated, head turning, voice deep and soft and seductive and strange. The little boy looked deep into the eyes of this strange man unlike any other grown-up he had ever seen, and decided that he was most unusual…but he was not afraid.

"Is that why you're here? Are you here to teach me?" he asked, suddenly excited beyond his wildest dreams.

The man drew closer,
and nodded once with
a smile.

The little boy peered at him curiously. "I know you from my dreams. You're Raven Man aren't you. Why have you waited so long to come for me?" he asked. But the Raven Man only smiled with his eyes and gave a small hop from one foot to the other.

"Fly," came the voices, "fly," he heard them calling. And this time, as he took the Raven Man's hand, he knew he finally would.

4:44

Brian Gueyser is an author hailing from the Great Lakes. He enjoys sharing great meals with close friends, amazingly delicious cuisine, and the quiet embrace of Nature's gentle solitude. His favourite colour is green. *The Boy Who Dreamt Of Flying* is his second published work. For more information, please visit https://wherebooksdream.com

Tim Lockett started drawing at a very young age and early on, received many awards and local notoriety for his work. Tim's work has been used in billboards, print and media. Aside from his art, Tim also sings, acts, and models. This is Tim's first children's book that he has illustrated.